To my airport friend Sheila
with best wishes
[illegible] 7 August 2015

MACRUDD - KING OF OZ
A TRAGEDY

BookVenture Publishing LLC
1000 Country Lane Ste 300
Ishpeming MI 49849
www.bookventure.com
Hotline: 1(877) 276-9751
Fax: 1(877) 864-1686

Ordering Information:
Quantity sales. Special discounts are available on quantity purchases by corporations, associations, and others. For details, contact the publisher at the address above.

Printed in the United States of America

Library of Congress Control Number:		2015900756
ISBN-13:	Softcover	978-1-942703-04-4
	Pdf	978-1-942703-05-1
	ePub	978-1-942703-06-8
	Kindle	978-1-942703-07-5

Rev. date: 05/08/2015

MACRUDD - KING OF OZ
A TRAGEDY

Kevin O'Donnell

Illustrations by JEFF—www.geoffhook.com

Contents

List of Characters

MacRudd, King of Oz
Lady MacRudd, Queen of Oz
The Red Witch
The Black Swan
Winky Bill
Simon the Clean
The Earl of Midnight
Lady Gong
The Faceless Men

The Mad Monk
The Baron of Net Worth
The Mad Hatter
Lord Windbags
Lord Apeshit
The Parrot
Laurie the Fat Goat

The Comedian
The Admiral
The White Bishop
The Archbishop
Big Joe the Bean Counter
The Boat Stopper
The Schoolboy Smartarse
The Sundowner

The Naughty Unionist
Mark the Angry
Bob the Blow-in

The Twig Man
The Pilbara Princess
The Turncoat Slipper
The Cardinal
Dr Green
The Browns (The Fairies at the Bottom of the Garden)
The Princess's Children
The Rich Mynahs
The Polluters
The Scientists
The Deniers
The Ambulance Chasers
The Stolen Ones
The Public Servants
The Reptiles
The People
The Big Dog and his Puppies

The Three Witches
The Old Kings:

- The Godfather
- The Squire
- The Sliver Bodgie
- The Master Blaster
- Honest John

Factors and Events

The MacRudd Persona

The Carbon Tax

The Climate

The Apology

The Mining Tax

Ditch the Witch

The Pink Batts

The Infrastructure Spending

Prologue

Enter the Godfather, a tall, imposing, ghostly figure, with a halo above his head.

Ah, to be king once more
I was, in mine own age
in those great days of yore
and I still maintain the rage

To have occupied the throne
to hold those levers of power
and been so rudely overthrown
the taste is still so sour

To reign for three mere years
and know it's up to you
with no brains among your peers
and support that's never true

With witches in the background
rooting for their own
with that horrible sound
as they cackle, hiss and groan

Faceless Men are all around
and Reptiles twist the news
all fury piss and sound
as they vomit out their boos

The burdens of the crown
can crush the very best
and bring them cruelly down
with blood upon their breast

So now we have MacRudd
in triumph he strides the stage
can he survive the mud
and bring a better age?

But has a wicked spell
been cast by witches three?
will MacRudd rule wise and well?
attend and you will see

ACT 1
THE NEW KING

Scene 1
The Palace Grounds

Three witches hustle in, in earnest conversation. Witch 1 is wearing overalls and a hard hat. Witch 2 is wearing a black suit and carrying a placard with 'Ambulance Chasers—No Win, No Fee' in large letters. Witch 3 is in casual clothes and carrying a lantern, with a pale light.

Witch 1

Phase 1 of our plan is run
Our plan is halfway done

Witch 2

Patience is now the key
My dear, what do you foresee? [to Witch 3]

Witch 3

MacRudd, he will not last
he's just a bleeding upstart
he belongs in the past
nothing but piss and fart

Witch 1

Fair is foul and foul is fair
MacRudd won't last three years

he'll cause strife everywhere
and prove true all our fears

Witch 2

That's when our Red will win
MacRudd will be outcast
consigned to the history bin
a relic of the past

Witch 3

Let's mix our wicked brew
then watch it all come true

Scene 2
The Throne Room

There is merriment at the palace, the air is full of triumph. MacRudd is surrounded by his troops.

The Black Swan

MacRudd is the new king. All hail King MacRudd. [cheers and great joy abound]

MacRudd

We have just routed the old king, Honest John, and banished him to the outer suburbs in disgrace. We even beat him up in his own stronghold.

Lady MacRudd

It was all because of you, my wonderful king. You are the victor, our hero. You were superb.

MacRudd [surveying his surroundings]

This palace has seen better days. We must bring it up to standard. It is so like Honest John—My God, how ironic! Even his closest courtiers and cousins didn't believe that any more. My lady queen, have this palace modernised, so it is fit for the new royal family. Lots of splendid new mirrors, so the king can look at himself as he goes about his business. Hmm, it's good to be the king.

The Black Swan

Lord Mac..

MacRudd

You may call me 'Your Majesty', my dear Swan.

The Black Swan [bows]

Thank you your majesty. Your majesty, we have much to do. It is fitting for you to celebrate with your subjects, but the rest of us should get to work. There is much to do to repair the damage that Oz has suffered of late.

MacRudd

Yes, get on with it Swan. And send the Red Witch to me. I need to consult with her.

Exit the Black Swan.

The Red Witch [enters and curtsies]

Your Majesty.

MacRudd

Ah, there you are my special witch. Your prediction was right. I am king. And you are the first of my subjects. When I am absent from Oz, spreading the message throughout the world, you shall deputise for me. What say you?

The Red Witch

I am immensely honoured, your majesty.

MacRudd

Now my favourite witch, what of the vanquished? Honest John is finished, is he not?

The Red Witch

Yes, my liege. Completely destroyed, even in his home town. His forces are defeated and demoralised. They are looking for a leader, and will probably re-form around the Comedian, in the hope that he will rebuild the House of Ming. But I doubt that he will.

MacRudd

What? Surely the Comedian is their only possible leader?

The Red Witch

You might think so my liege, but there are questions about his ticker. Many in the Ming House expected him to knife Honest John, just like the Master Blaster did to the Silver Bodgie. But he simply didn't have the cojones.

MacRudd [giggling]

Well, if not him, who?

The Red Witch

They are a rabble, my liege. I expect there to be a contest between the two biggest egos in the country, the Admiral and the Baron of Net Worth. The Admiral will probably win.

MacRudd

Then we must prepare for that prospect, and make his life as uncomfortable as we can.
Now, I'll need a speech for the apology to the dispossessed, and one to take to the climate change conference. I'll show the world we're up for the important issues of our times.

Scene 3
The Throne Room

MacRudd and the Red Witch are discussing the developments in the House of Ming

MacRudd

My dear witch, you were right again. I can't believe how quickly the Comedian caved in.

The Red Witch

Most people had expected him to be as tough as the Master Blaster, but there's a huge difference. The Blaster had a real killer instinct, hard and ruthless. Look at the way he knocked off the Silver Bodgie. The Comedian's nothing but a cream puff. He had the chance to roll Honest John, but squibbed it.

MacRudd

And we've got the jump on the Admiral. Witch, you're nearly as good as me. And it's me the people love!

The Red Witch

Yes, your majesty. You must be pleased at how well the Apology to the Stolen Ones went down. Now you have the climate change conference to charm, and then the Chinese. The first king of Oz to speak Mandarin. You'll have them eating out of your hand.

MacRudd

Plus, we've got the Admiral on the run. I've laid down the law to the Public Service. Making them work around the clock, producing work overnight. The place is really humming. I'll leave the running of the place to you while I'm at the climate conference and visiting China and Japan. But don't forget I'll be on the phone every day.

Scene 4
The Throne Room

MacRudd is holding court, talking with the Red Witch.

MacRudd

My dear witch. The Admiral is sinking. We have proven our superiority over him. The People are clearly recognising how much better I am than him.

The Red Witch

Yes, my liege, you are supreme. The Admiral's hours are numbered. There is much consternation in the House of Ming. I predict that the Admiral will very shortly be replaced by the Baron of Net Worth.

MacRudd

Ha, the Baron is the only person in the land who has more money than I have. We must destroy him, just as we did with the Admiral.

The Red Witch

He will be different from the Admiral, my liege. He will most likely support our climate change program. He'll take a more subtle approach, and be harder to differentiate ourselves from.

MacRudd

Indeed witch, but remember, I'm so much smarter than anyone else in the land. He can't compete with me. [admiring himself in one of the large mirrors]

Simon the Clean rushes in.

MacRudd

My dear Simon. You have news? Tell me, what is the latest gossip on the House of Ming?

Simon the Clean

Yes my liege. Good news. The House of Ming has tossed the Admiral overboard. The Baron of Net Worth is their new leader.

MacRudd

Excellent. Just as we suspected they would. We have the jump on them. I'll consult with the Faceless Men on how to demolish the Baron. Send them in.

The Red Witch and Simon the Clean exit.

Scene 5
The Throne Room

MacRudd, the Red Witch and the Black Swan are deep in discussion about the Global Financial Crisis.

MacRudd

This crisis has me concerned. It is causing havoc all around the world.

The Red Witch

My liege, we are very privileged here in Oz. We are well protected from the worst of the crisis, but we must safeguard our economy. What think you, Swan?

The Black Swan

The world's economies will slow down, and that will affect our exports. In turn, that will increase our unemployment. One of our options is to stimulate the economy, and create jobs through government programs.

The Red Witch

If we do that, it will increase the deficit, but as a nation, we'll be better off. Lower unemployment, more business activity. We'd avoid going into recession while the rest of the world suffers.

MacRudd

It would have to be well targeted, and provide lots of jobs.

The Black Swan

There are many infrastructure programs crying out for money. What about upgrading/refurbishing schools, roads, new school halls and gymnasiums, that sort of thing. Helping householders to become more efficient with their energy use.

MacRudd

Insulation. Cheap insulation in their ceilings. No, let's make it free for all but the very rich. Pink batts in the ceilings. Oh yes, that's the key. My reign will be forever remembered for the

Pink Batts program! Send in the Oil. You know, Swan—the Oil of Midnight. [chuckles at his own little joke]

The Black Swan exits, and the Earl of Midnight enters.

MacRudd

Oh here you are Oil. I have a job for you. I want to stimulate the economy by installing Pink Batts in every roof cavity. We'll create lots of jobs, and help people to use less power. Fewer Blue Sky Mines. [giggles] Sometimes I even surprise myself with my brilliance. Less carbon usage—oh, this is a great part of my legacy.

The Earl of Midnight [earnestly]

Do you want me to prepare a discussion paper for the party room to consider?

MacRudd

Jesus Christ no! Fair suck of the sauce bottle. Don't waste your time with those fucking cattle. It is already policy. I have decreed! I just want you to prepare an implementation program. Have it on my desk by 4.00 am tomorrow, and I'll sign it off. I want this operating within a week.

The Earl of Midnight

Yes, my liege. [bows and exits]

The Red Witch

My liege, aren't you being a bit hard on the public service—and even the ministry? They find it hard that you want them all to work throughout the night.

MacRudd

What bullshit. We have major works to do, programs to run. There's no time for fucking around. Either those rat-fuckers perform or they're out the door. And that goes for cabinet as much as anyone. I mean to leave a great legacy for my people.

Scene 6
The Red Witch's Office

The Red Witch is conferring with the Black Swan, Simon the Clean, Lady Gong, Winky Bill and the Earl of Midnight.

Simon the Clean

But the king is such hard work, witch. He yells and screams and swears at everyone, demands everything be on his desk in twelve hours or less, then doesn't look at it for months. The only thing that went through quickly was the Pink Batts program—and that has disaster written all over it.

The Black Swan

And the only time anything gets approved, witch, is when he's big-noting himself around the world, when you work through the paperwork and move things along. He's proving to be a major disappointment.

Winky Bill

The king is becoming a real problem for us. His popularity is still OK, but it's dropping slowly. That episode in the USA at a strip club is no good for his image. And the stories about his bad temper and rude treatment of staff are gaining traction.

Lady Gong

The good news is that we're still well in front in the polls. The Baron hasn't laid a glove on us yet.

The Earl of Midnight

Our climate change legislation is nearly ready to introduce. I'll have it to you in the next few days, witch, so you can give it a tick before the king returns.

The Red Witch

Yes, and we have the Baron skewered on this. He's committed the House of Ming to support it. What name did we decide on?

Lady Gong

We're calling it the ETS—Emissions Trading Scheme. Quite a few of the business community are on board. Not wildly excited, but on board. The Baron has nowhere to run. Like a rabbit in the headlights!

Simon the Clean

The even better news is that they have no other leader in their camp. There's Big Joe the Bean Counter—big man but a real lightweight. And then there's the Mad Monk. [laughter all round]

The Black Swan

Imagine the Mad Monk as leader. Not even a mob as dysfunctional as the House of Ming would want the Monk fronting them.

The meeting broke up amongst much hilarity.

Scene 7
The Throne Room

Corks are popping as the king and his retinue celebrate the demise of the Baron of Net Worth, and the surprise announcement that the Mad Monk was now the leader of the House of Ming. The TV news is running in the background

MacRudd

My dear witch, this time you were wrong. We were all wrong. Who in their right mind would have thought that they'd turn to the Mad Monk? He is their worst possible leader.

Simon the Clean

The People will never warm to him. He's crazy. He takes advice from the much-hated Cardinal, and describes climate change science as crap. An everlasting loser.

MacRudd

The House of Ming are so rattled, they've chosen the wrong man. I'll rout him and hold the throne for as long as I like. I expected them to go for Big Joe.

The Red Witch

Big Joe might be big physically, but he's another lightweight. The way he campaigned for the job, you could tell he was soft.

The Earl of Midnight

Look, the Baron is talking at a press conference. It'll be interesting to hear what he has to say. [turns up the volume]

The Baron of Net Worth [on the TV]

He [the Mad Monk] himself in just four or five months publicly advocated the blocking of the ETS, the passing of the ETS, the amending of the ETS and if the amendments were satisfactory, passing it, and now the blocking of it. His only redeeming virtue in this remarkable lack of conviction is that every time he announced a new position to me he would preface it with "Mate, mate, I know I am a bit of a weather vane on this, but . . ."

MacRudd [roaring with laughter]

And that's what we're up against. A toast, my friends. To the Mad Monk. Long may he lead the House of Ming.

And everyone present drank the toast and laughed and celebrated long into the night

Scene 8
The Palace Grounds

It's Sunday, about lunch time. Several senior Public Servants are standing around, together with Simon the Clean, Lady Gong, Winky Bill, the Earl of Midnight, and the Faceless Men.

Lady Gong

This is ridiculous. The king called us all here at 4.00 am, on the basis that we were all required for a big talk fest, and we've just been waiting around for hours. I need some lunch.

The Earl of Midnight

I need some sleep. MacRudd does murder sleep.

Winky Bill

He's only got the Red Witch and the Black Swan in there, and we're all just wasting our time. We all have work to do, he sets up impossible deadlines, then demands we all hang around here like naughty kids, and just keeps us waiting. What a prick!

Simon the Clean

We should get the Earl to call his band to come and put on a bit of entertainment for us. Could someone see if the Palace kitchen can dig up some food for us? I'm starving.

The Earl of Midnight

This is so boring and degrading. If only we could organise some form of entertainment.

Lady Gong

No Earl, we don't need you to sing for us. Please!

The Earl of Midnight

No no no. I wouldn't sing here without my buddies, and a large fee. I was rather thinking about lawn bowls or croquet, something suited to all these lawns—and guaranteed to go on for hours. Rather than just waiting here all day doing nothing!

ACT 2
THE TROOPS ARE REVOLTING

Scene 1
Backroom at the Palace

The Faceless Men have gathered. They are growing concerned

Faceless Man 1

This is starting to remind me of how things were with the Godfather.

Faceless Man 2

Was his reign ever this dysfunctional?

Faceless Man 3

It was never this bad when the Godfather was king. At least he made decisions and got on with things. He had real vision.

Faceless Man 1

Indeed he did, But remember that our leader before the Godfather said of him "Yes, he'll take you to power, but he'll take you out again just as fast." I fear the same thing is happening here.

Faceless Man 3

Mark the Angry said the same thing about MacRudd.

Faceless Man 2

Remember that the Godfather was deposed after only three years. Could that happen here?

Faceless Man 1

But the king is still very popular with the People. Much more popular than the Mad Monk.

Faceless Man 3

The question is how long can we keep the People in the dark about the king's behaviour and his procrastination. That's a huge problem. If word gets out, his popularity will plummet and we might have to consider the unthinkable.

Faceless Man 2

We are lucky the Mad Monk is leading the Mings. If they had a real leader we'd be in trouble. Look at his opposition to the ETS. All over the place. The People will never warm to him.

Scene 2
The Throne Room

MacRudd is pacing up and down between rows of files and documents. The piles are about his height, and there are rows of them. Full length mirrors have been installed at the end of each row, so he can admire himself at every turn.

MacRudd [coming out from behind a row of files]

What's going on around here? This is a fucking disaster. Get me the fucking Oil. Get his arse in here . . . Now!

Public Servant

The Oil? Who is the fu..

MacRudd

The fucking Earl of course. The Earl of Midnight. Don't you dopey cunts know anything? Am I fated to be the only person around here with any brains? [preening himself in the large mirror opposite his desk] Well . . . . of course I am. Silly question, your majesty. [continues smiling at his reflection, then turns to the aide]. Now fuck off and do it!. Don't you stand around when I give you an order, you lazy prick. Have him here in half an hour.

Public Servant

But, your majesty, he's in Tasmania, trying to make peace in the timber industry.

MacRudd

I don't give a flying fuck what he and his fellow tree huggers are doing down there. Get him on the next plane and get his arse in here. Pronto!

Public Servant rushes out.

MacRudd [glances at the pile of documents on his desk, on the floor, covering his lounge suite and chairs. Sighs]

Why is it always up to me? Yes, I know, I'm the only one who can do it. No-one else is smart enough to do it all. Can't let anything happen without my personal sign-off. Such is the price I must pay for being the most beautiful, talented and intelligent person in the kingdom. [gazes longingly at his reflection in the mirror]

Scene 3
The Throne Room

Twelve hours later, the Earl of Midnight is ushered in.

The Earl

You wanted to see me, my liege?

MacRudd

Yes, what took you so fucking long? I wanted you here twelve hours ago.

The Earl

I came as soon as I heard, but I've been cooling my heels in your outer office for eight hours, waiting for you to find time to see me. I was sorting out an agreement in Tasmania. Peace in our time in the timber industry. The Fairies at the Bottom of the Garden are livid with envy. The great Dr Green is now truly green—how good's that? [chortling] They're fucking green with envy! The Browns are green.

MacRudd

Listen to me, you greasy fuckwit. I've just heard about a series of disasters in my home province. It's those fucking Pink Batts. People installing them are dying.

The Earl

Oh shit, has it got that bad? That's even worse than I thought.

MacRudd [screaming with fury]

YOU ALREADY KNEW IT WAS BAD? YOU FUCKING KNEW IT WAS BAD. WHY DIDN'T YOU TELL ME, YOU USELESS CUNT?

The Earl

There was a report about all sorts of safety problems. The whole implementation was a fuck-up.

MacRudd

WHY DIDN'T YOU FUCKING TELL ME?

The Earl [clears his throat]

Err, I did. I sent you a report and a submission six months ago. [looks around] Ah, it would probably be in this pile [buries himself in a pile of documents halfway along the wall] Yes, here it is, dated . . .

MacRudd

BUT YOU COULD HAVE TOLD ME—YOU KNOW, BY TALKING TO ME!

The Earl [throws up his hands in exasperation]

No-one can ever get to talk to you, not unless you actually summon them into your presence. I emailed you seven or eight times. I tried calling you dozens of times. Then I tried to get your chief of staff, but he told me you haven't been on speaking terms for months. You're impossible to get through to!

MacRudd

That useless rat-fucker! He was late for a meeting one morning. Claimed he hadn't slept in three days. Soft and weak, so I froze him out. Hmm . . . . . . Well, too late to do anything about the Pink Batts now. Stop all installations, put out a statement of regret and blame it on hiccups in the public service. Now fuck off, and let me get on with running the country.

The Earl exits, shaking his head and muttering to himself.

Scene 4
Backroom at the Palace

The Faceless Men are pacing around in a tizz. They have been joined by Winky Bill and Simon the Clean.

Faceless Man 3

How could it have come to this. We are in real trouble.

Faceless Man 2

The People have lost faith in us. The climate conference was a waste of time, and made the king look like a useless tool. He's managed to piss off every country in Asia.

Faceless Man 3

The ETS is not going to get through, and everyone now knows about his bad behaviour and policy paralysis. The Mad Monk has him on the run. And now this Pink Batts catastrophe.

Faceless Man 1

Is it time to seriously consider tossing him out? I know that's unheard of with a king this early in his reign.

Faceless Man 3

Did you know that Ming was the last king to voluntarily vacate the throne? All the rest have been overthrown, either by their enemies or their own house. They won't let go by themselves. But none have been dethroned by their own side in less than three years.

Faceless Man 1

The House of Ming are massing their troops, and the people are swinging in behind them—even with the Mad Monk in charge. We'll have to go into battle with them soon. Can we win with the king in charge?

Faceless Man 2

If not the king, then who?

Faceless Man 3

The Red Witch is our best bet. She's intelligent, gets things done. Without her, the king's procrastination would have ground the country to a complete halt by now. We need him to be overseas more, so we can implement at least some of our policies.

Faceless Man 1

Yes, but the problem with that is that he gets up the noses of everyone he comes across, and the Reptiles are having a field day, ridiculing the king—and all of us.

Faceless Man 3

Is there anyone else to replace him with? Is the Red Witch our only hope? I know she's our best bet, but will she agree to knife him? If she does, she'll inevitably be seen to have blood on her hands.

Faceless Man 2

I suggest that we quietly canvass our team, and see where the numbers lie. Winky and Simon, can you carefully sound out the witch, and see what she thinks about it?

Winky Bill and Simon the Clean nod, and they all exit.

Scene 5
The Red Witch's Office

The Red Witch is working through a pile of papers on her desk, when Simon the Clean and Winky Bill enter.

The Red Witch

Oh hello gentlemen. I'm working on all the files from the king's office while he's off at the United Nations. There's such a lot to do.

Winky Bill [clearing his throat]

Yes witch, that's one of the things we wanted to talk to you about.

The Red Witch

Are you offering to give me a hand? I couldn't accept it. The king only very reluctantly agreed to me working through the files while he's away. He'd go off his nut if I delegated any of it to anyone else. You know what he's like.

Simon the Clean

No witch, that wasn't what he meant. Can we speak in confidence?

The Red Witch

Yes you can. [frowns] Why am I worried about what you're going to say?

Winky Bill

We've just had a meeting with the Faceless Men. They're very worried about the king, and are sounding out the troops about a coup.

The Red Witch

What? A coup? I couldn't have a bar of that. No, no, no. I'm loyal to the king.

Winky Bill

Look, witch. The king is sinking fast. If we aren't careful, he'll take us all down with him. His flaws will be the end of him—and of us.

The Red Witch

No, I'm sticking tight with the king.

Simon the Clean

OK, we respect that. Just keep it in mind, OK? If it gets any worse, there'll be a move against him anyway. We won't be able to stop it.

Simon the Clean and Winky Bill exit. The Red Witch sits with her head in her hands.

Scene 6
The MacRudd Chateau

MacRudd and Lady MacRudd are talking confidentially.

MacRudd

Oh, woe is me! I am surrounded by pygmies, idiots and imbeciles. They find a way to . . . foul up everything. I have all the bright ideas, and they find ways to stuff them up. I can't trust them to do anything right.

Lady MacRudd

Don't worry, my love. You're still the best and the brightest. Your offsiders are only jealous. And besides, you can easily thrash that upstart Monk. The people love you, not the Monk.

MacRudd

I know, I know. Not being able to trust anybody means that I have to do it all myself, so the paperwork builds up to a ridiculous level. Even for me, it's a huge burden.

Lady MacRudd

I feel safe knowing that you're doing it all.

MacRudd

And all the while, I just know that those ungrateful bastards are plotting against me—not just the Mad Monk and his cronies, but some of our own house as well.

Lady MacRudd

Surely not your old colleague the Black Swan, or the loyal Red Witch?

MacRudd

Probably not, but it's got to the stage where I can't be certain. My only course is to not trust anyone. No-one. Except for you of course. You're my only one.

Scene 7
On the King's Plane

The king and the Black Swan are visiting their old province, one of the few remaining areas where the king remains very popular. They are discussing the threat posed by the Mad Monk.

MacRudd

I have my ear to the ground, Swan. I know that there are rumblings in our house, and the peasants are revolting. There was even a cartoon showing me like the King of Id, with someone holding a placard saying 'The King is a Fink'.

The Black Swan

No, your majesty. When the polls drop, there is always a small fringe element that turns into Chicken Little, and runs around crying out 'The sky is falling'. But the troops are solidly behind you.

MacRudd

That's what worries me, Swan. They're behind me all right—with knives in their hands, waiting for their opportunity to kill me—just like Caesar at the Forum. Are you my Brutus, Swan?

The Black Swan

That's paranoid talk, your majesty. Take it from me, there is no plot against you. The troops are loyal. Nothing can happen without the witch and me being part of it—and we're not!

MacRudd

Swan, promise me that you'll always support me. We go a long way back.

The Black Swan

I will not stab you in the back. If it ever comes to the stage where the numbers are against you, I'll tell you to your face. Man to man.

MacRudd

No, Swan. Promise me that you'll always support me! I demand it. I am your king!

The Black Swan

You know that I support you. All I'll say is that, if it's all over, I'll tell you, and let you move on with dignity. And now, it's not over. You are the king, and you'll destroy the Mad Monk.

ACT 3
THE COUP

Scene 1
Backroom at the Palace

The Faceless Men are hard at work, sifting the mood of the People, whispering among themselves and the king's team, making phone calls and crunching the numbers. They are carrying reams of loose papers.

Faceless Man 1

The polls are terrible and getting worse. The king is dead in the water. He's being outpolled by the Mad Monk for fuck's sake. We have crisis after crisis, fiasco after fiasco. The Pink Batts have been a disaster. And there's no sign of it slowing down.

Faceless Man 2

The king is gone. His reign is over. We have to act. Our private polling is even worse than the public ones.

Faceless Man 3

If we don't have a palace coup, then we are toast. The Mad Monk will oust him, and we'll be in the wilderness. We have no option. We must act.

Faceless Man 1

OK, we're all agreed. We have to topple him. We have the numbers, but we must have a new monarch we can rally the troops around. We need the Red Witch on board. We have Simon the Clean and Winky Bill. The Earl looks like he's with us, but we need the witch. She is the only one who can change the game and defeat the Mad Monk.

Faceless Man 2

If it must be done, then best it be done quickly.

Faceless Man 3

So how do we convince her? She has her own mind.

Faceless Man 2

We'll have Simon and Winky talk to her. They can show her our polls, and tell her we have the numbers comfortably. Once she understands that we're history without her, and that we can win with her, she'll have no choice. She will join us. She must join us.

Faceless Man1 pulls out his phone and calls Winky Bill.

Scene 2
The Red Witch's Office

The Red Witch is working her way through piles of documents on her desk, when Winky Bill and Simon the Clean are ushered into her office.

The Red Witch [smiling]

Hello gentlemen. [stops smiling] Uh Oh. I'm not sure I like the looks on your faces. Tell me the news.

Winky Bill

You know how bad the published polls are. Our own polling is even worse. If we stay with the king, we'll all be routed. Thrown into the wilderness for a very long time. If we don't get rid of him we're doomed.

Simon the Clean

There is one piece of positive news. One way we can turn back the Mad Monk. Only one. A change of monarch. Only one monarch can save us—you! The polls say you will trounce the Mad Monk.

The Red Witch

No, I can't do it.

Winky Bill

For all our sakes, you must. Here, look at the numbers. [produces a sheaf of papers] Look, if he stays, we are a beaten rabble. If you lead us, we triumph. We slay the Monk. For the sake of our troops—they'll be totally destroyed. How could you let this happen to them?

The Red Witch

I see what you mean, but I can't challenge him. I won't challenge him. I refuse to have his blood on my hands.

Winky Bill

You won't need to. The numbers are strongly against him. Once he knows the score, he'll step down, and you won't have to fight him. The Black Swan will tell him, and he'll withdraw.

The Red Witch

Can you be certain of that?

Simon the Clean and Winky Bill [in unison]

Yes, we guarantee it!

The Red Witch [breathes heavily]

OK. On that basis I'm in. I'm not happy about it, but I'm in.

Scene 3
The Black Swan's Office

The Black Swan is also knee deep in paperwork, when Winky Bill and Simon the Clean rush in.

The Black Swan

OK, something's going on. What is it?

Simon the Clean

The king is history. The published polls are bad. Our own polls are worse. The troops are overwhelmingly in favour of changing the monarch. [holds out a sheaf of papers for Swan to look at]

Winky Bill

The good news is that, with the witch as leader, we can defeat the Monk, and stay in power. So here's where we need you.

The Black Swan

You want me to knife him? No, I won't do that.

Simon the Clean

You don't have to knife him. All you have to do is tell him the truth—that the troops are against him, that he doesn't have any real support. Didn't you tell us that, if he knows he's beaten, he'll step aside without a contest?

The Black Swan

Yes I did. He wouldn't want to fight and lose, so he'll step aside. Are you certain that the numbers are against him?

Winky Bill

Absolutely certain. He has no support. Look at these numbers. [handing over the sheaf]. Best to let him down gently. Can you tap him on the shoulder? The witch is ready to take over, but doesn't want to fight him for the throne. She'd like to keep him in the tent as roving ambassador, where he could still be part of the house, and freely roam the world.

The Black Swan [sighs]

OK, it has to be done. I'll go and see him now.

Scene 4
The Throne Room

MacRudd is pacing up and down between rows of files, all about his own height. The Black Swan enters.

The Black Swan

Are you here, my liege?

MacRudd [emerges]

Oh, it's you Swan. Who let you in? What the fuck do you want?

The Black Swan

There was no-one in the outer office, so I let myself in. A word, my liege. You remember our conversation on the royal plane a month ago, when we discussed the possibility of the numbers falling against you?

MacRudd [steps back, a look of alarm on his face]

What? What is this? Have you come to knife me, you Brutus? You traitor!

The Black Swan

No my liege. Never! You know I support you. But I told you I would let you know if the numbers turned against you. And they have. Badly. The members of our house are massing against you. The numbers are very bad. Very bad. If it came to a fight, you'd lose.

MacRudd [shocked]

Is it that bad Swan? Is there no hope?

The Black Swan

It is that bad my liege. There is no hope. The numbers are very firm. My advice is to leave with dignity.

MacRudd

Is it that fucking witch? Is she behind this?

The Black Swan

No my liege. She is loyal, and would not oppose you, and will accept the crown only after you depart. Plus, she values your abilities, and would seek to keep you in the fold, as roving ambassador.

MacRudd

Of course she would, the fucking bitch. She'll live to regret this treachery. You mark my words. So full of envy. She's always hated me, been jealous of me. She's been white-anting me since I became king. [pauses] OK, tell her I'll abdicate as king, and will accept the position as roving ambassador. But I'm not happy, Swan. Not happy at all! Fucking sorceress!

Scene 5
The Red Witch's Office

There is a quiet, sober party going on, with the Red Witch presiding. A couple of staffers are drinking champagne, but there is no merriment.

Winky Bill

The king is dead. God save the Queen. A toast to the new queen.

The Red Witch

Thank you Winky. I don't feel good about deposing MacRudd, and I'm glad that he left quietly. Plus, I fear that we have a huge challenge before us, to defeat the Mad Monk. [The Black Swan enters] Ah, here is the Swan. Thank you Swan, for talking to MacRudd. I assume he's disappointed?

The Black Swan [bows]

Yes, majesty. Congratulations by the way. He's more than disappointed. Bitter and vitriolic, you might say. There are many good haters in the history of our house, and he's right up there with the best of them.

Faceless Man 3 [enters]

MacRudd has refused interviews, but has just released a press statement. He says he congratulates the new queen on her coronation, and will be happy to work with her as roving ambassador. Nothing else.

Winky Bill

Nothing else? That's a very bald statement. My god, he's extremely bitter. He's got such an ego that he really thinks he's superior to us all, and he'll never forgive. He'll be a running problem for us to deal with.

Faceless Man 2

Well we can't cry over spilt milk. We have to make every post a winner now, and roll that bastard Monk.

Faceless Man 1

I can't believe how negative he is. His only policy is to oppose absolutely everything. The only word he knows is 'No'.

The Red Witch

What are the Reptiles saying?

Simon the Clean

They were at first surprised, particularly that it was done so quickly. The loudmouths are saying that we all have blood on our hands, and the Mad Monk has taken up that line. He's repeating it over and over, as nauseam. As he does.

Winky Bill

He can only keep one simple thought in his head at a time, so that's all he can do. Repeat it over and over.

ACT 4
THE RED WITCH IS QUEEN

Scene 1
The Palace Grounds

The witches enter, cackling merrily. They are all dressed in black, witches hats and all. One of them is still carrying a placard with 'Ambulance chasers. No Win—No Fee' in large letters. One is carrying a hard hat in her hand. The third still carries the lantern, this time with a brilliant light.

Witch 1

Success, she's done it
the Red Witch is queen
our plan has won it
a triumph it has been

Witch 2

But what will happen now?
what will be her fate
a woman at the prow
will bring forth lots of hate

Witch 3

My joy is tinged with fear
The Monk will carp and stir
and what is worse—oh dear
MacRudd is after her

Scene 2
The Throne Room

There are muted celebrations at the palace. The Faceless Men have crowned the Red Witch as Queen, and she is wearing her robes. The Black Swan is looking solemn.

The Black Swan

Congratulations my queen. It is wonderful to see you on the throne. But we must beware. The Mad Monk is not our only enemy. There will be trouble from our own side.

Simon the Clean

Surely not one of our own? Who is this Judas? It can't be . . . . .

The Black Swan

Yes, it's definitely MacRudd. He still craves the throne. He hasn't given up hopes of returning to the palace in triumph. He's bitter and vindictive. He'll do everything he can to bring you down.

The Red Witch

Even though I appointed him my roving ambassador, to keep him inside the tent?

The Black Swan

I understand, your majesty. You'd rather have him inside the tent pissing out than outside the tent pissing in. But MacRudd will piss on everyone, inside or out. He's obsessed with himself. Doesn't care what damage he causes.

Winky Bill

Just what we don't need. When we should be using all our energy to fight the Mad Monk, we have to deal with that bastard on our own side.

The Red Witch

Never mind him now. We have a major battle coming up with the Mad Monk. We must prepare for that.

Simon the Clean

Yes majesty, you know the Mad Monk doesn't believe in climate change. Just the other day he described it as crap. If we go ahead with the ETS, we can make him look stupid.

The Red Witch

Yes, he's lined up with the Deniers and the Polluters. The whole kingdom will see how out of touch he is!

Scene 3
The MacRudd Chateau

MacRudd and Lady MacRudd are deep in conversation.

MacRudd

Yes my love, I'm getting good publicity about my performances as roving ambassador, and I know the Red Witch's weaknesses. My friends in the media are quietly placing a few negative stories about her and the way she runs the country. She'll regret the way she knifed me!

Lady MacRudd

With a few well-placed leaks to the press, she'll have her hands full taking the fight to the Mad Monk. If we do it right, she'll be so weakened that she'll lose that battle.

MacRudd

Yes, and then our house will turn to me to take over and lead them back to power. I'll vanquish the Red Witch and then destroy the Monk, and be more powerful than ever. Remember, my love, there was a little issue when she worked with the Ambulance Chasers. I'll drop that into the hands of the House of Ming. The Schoolboy Smartarse would love to get his teeth into that.

Scene 4
The Black Swan's Office

The Black Swan has just been named the world's greatest treasurer. He is celebrating with Lady Gong, the Earl of Midnight, Simon the Clean and Winky Bill.

The Black Swan

How good is this? Finally some recognition for the way we protected the Oz economy when the GFC hit. Our stimulus package kept us from going into recession like the rest of the world did. Oh, sweet karma.

Winky Bill

Great work Swan. Well deserved. The Mad Monk will be almost speechless.

Lady Gong

Almost . . . but not quite. He'll find something negative about it, don't you worry! But MacRudd will be the most pissed off about it. He'll think all the credit should go to him.

Simon the Clean

Right this minute, he'll be on the phone to his media mates, telling them it was all his doing—even though we all know it wasn't. The only idea he had was the Pink Batts [shudders]

Scene 5
MacRudd's Hotel Suite in New York

MacRudd is furious. He is talking on the phone.

MacRudd

But it was me. It happened when I was king. It was my decision. Fucking Swan. He couldn't count to ten without his fingers. World's greatest treasurer? World's greatest at claiming credit. And equal best at treachery. They should have given him an award for that. Him and the fucking witch!

[listens for a moment]—Yes, make sure you spell that out. I should have won the award. They're all economic illiterates. DAMAGE THEM AS MUCH AS YOU CAN! And remember that story about the fucking Ambulance Chasers!

Scene 6
On the Hustings

The Red Witch is on stage, campaigning for the People's support. The Black Swan is standing behind her on one side, and Simon the Clean on the other. In the background are large posters showing the Old Kings, the Godfather, the Silver Bodgie and the Master Blaster. There is no poster of MacRudd.

The Red Witch

[channelling the Godfather] Men and women of Oz. We are here to bring greatness to our country. We have saved our economy, we have improved education, health and the fortunes of our people. We have made huge progress in reconciliation. We have enhanced our standing in the world. We have detailed plans to improve our environment. We will shortly introduce our emissions trading scheme, which will be a world leader. There will be no carbon tax. I repeat—NO CARBON TAX!

Scene 7
The Palace on Showdown Night

The Red Witch and her team are nervously watching the count on TV. All her people are there, except MacRudd.

Faceless Man 1

That total arsehole MacRudd. He backstabbed us and white-anted us at every turn. He did everything he possibly could to stop us winning. Arrogant, self-obsessed prick. He'll live in Oz history in the same category as that old bald bastard from the old days.

Faceless Man 3

So-called Honest John? Lazarus with a triple bypass?

Faceless Man 1

No, stupid! The one before the Godfather. That old prick lied and leaked and backstabbed everybody until he got the top job. Then he was a laughing stock, and the Godfather rolled right over him. Jesus it was good!

Faceless Man 3

Just like fucking MacRudd. No wonder he hasn't turned up here tonight. I'd kill him with my bare hands.

Winky Bill

That would not do at all. We'd then finish up with someone from the Ming House in his seat, and we can't afford that.

The Red Witch

That's right. If we hold on, I'll still have to keep him as my roving ambassador. UURGGHH!

Simon the Clean

Meanwhile, can we just keep in front of the Mad Monk and hold onto power?

Winky Bill

If we do, it'll be by the skin of our teeth, and even then we'll have to mortgage our souls to the Browns. Their Dr Green drives a hard bargain.

The Red Witch

Dr Green is more likely to go with us than the Mad Monk. That'll help us in the provinces. But it's the inner territories where we need support from the unaligned.

Faceless Man 2

Oh shit. Are we going to have to negotiate with the Mad Hatter, Apeshit and Windbags. Don't like our chances there.

The Red Witch

Well, there's no other option. I have to talk to them—and do a better job than the Mad Monk.

Faceless Man 3 [glumly]

Lots of luck, your majesty

Simon the Clean

Let's look at the numbers. Hmm, it's line ball between us and the House of Ming. We need at least two of the unaligned, and I can't imagine the Mad Hatter going with us. He'll line up with the Monk for sure. They deserve each other.

Faceless Man 2

What can we offer the other two? Their territories are closer to the Mad Monk's than ours as well.

The Red Witch

So, I'll have to persuade them . . .

Scene 8
The Throne Room

The queen and her team are anxiously watching the TV, as the unaligned, one by one, declare their positions. The Faceless Men are drinking heavily.

Faceless Man 2

Jesus Christ. These turkeys are going to take all week. Why do they have to ramble on and put everyone to sleep. Just tell us yes or no, us or them!

The Earl of Midnight

Let 'em go. It's their time in the sun. It's the nature of any political animal to speak forever when they get the chance.

Faceless Man 1

Yeah, but as soon as this is over, they'll be back in Nowheresville.

Simon the Clean

Not those who finish up making the government. They'll be in the spotlight for the next three years. What think you, majesty?

The Red Witch

I see the Mad Hatter is going first. He's likely to line up with the Monk—they are both the same kind of crazy.

Winky Bill

In that case we'll need both Apeshit and Windbags. That's a long shot.

The Red Witch

Don't be too sure. I think we're in with a chance. I got the impression that they weren't impressed with the Monk. He was prepared to offer them whatever they wanted if they could make him king. He's so desperate that he'd do anything, and it seemed that Windbags and Apeshit lost any respect they ever had for him.

Faceless Man 3

OK, so we're still in this. We might still make it.

Faceless Man 2

The Mad Hatter is still raving on. Hang on, he's about to . . . oh fuck! He's going with the Monk. [pours himself another drink]

A melancholy settles over the gathering, as they await their fortune.

Scene 9
The Throne Room

Many hours later. The same people are still watching the same TV. Ties have been loosened, tempers are short, desks and the floor are littered with empties, words are being slurred. The Red Witch alone is focused on the TV.

Faceless Man 1

Fucking Windbags has earned his title. He's been going for longer than the Mad Hatter. If he goes with the Monk we're fucked. Is he getting there finally?

Faceless Man 3

Looks like it. Just a minute . . . . YESSS! One all. Now it's up to that prick Apeshit.

Scene 10
The Throne Room

Several hours later. The same people are present, some in very bad repair, draped over the furniture. Faceless Man 2 is comatose on a sofa, as others argue loudly about what to do if Lord Apeshit chooses to support the Mad Monk. The Red Witch is working quietly at her desk, with one eye on the TV. Faceless Man 1 is the only one watching the TV intently.

Simon the Clean [wanders over to Faceless Man 1]

Well comrade, as the Godfather would have said, some of your colleagues can't hold their liquor. They wouldn't have lasted five minutes back in the old days. Is Apeshit still going? Is he trying for a world record filibuster or something?

Faceless Man 1

Some of the Reptiles in the audience have dozed off. They'll be shitty if they wake up and everyone has gone and they miss the story.

Simon the Clean

He's about to tell us . . . . YESSS!!! He's with us. Majesty, we have the numbers. You're still queen.You fucking beauty!!

The others wake up and leap out of their chairs. There is much yelling and the drinking resumes with a vengeance. Faceless

Man 2 half awakens and rolls off the sofa with a thud. He does not move.

The Red Witch [wearily]

Oh yes, we're still in power, but we'll have to juggle the numbers and keep a volatile majority from falling apart. Not to mention two oppositions, the Mad Monk on one hand, and MacRudd on the other.

Faceless Man 2 [stirs and belches]

Two oppositions?

The Red Witch [snapping]

I said not to mention the two oppositions. We'll hear enough of them anyway!

ACT 5
THE RED WITCH'S DOWNFALL

Scene 1
The Throne Room

The Red Witch, the Black Swan and their supporters are in a bad mood. Negotiations with the Fairies at the Bottom of the Garden have been tense and unproductive.

Faceless Man 2 [with a drink in his hand, and a bandage on his head]

Those fucking Fairies. They have no fucking idea! And Dr Green, he should know better. They said they'd support us, then they refuse to vote for the ETS. For fuck's sake, that's what the election was about!

Winky Bill

So where does that leave us now?

The Red Witch

They say they'll vote for a carbon tax. They conveniently forget that I promised there'd be no carbon tax. So we're left with breaking a solemn promise or doing nothing about climate change.

Faceless Man 1

We're screwed either way. Fucking Browns. Can't trust them as far as I could spit a rat. The Mad Monk will have a field day with that shit.

The Red Witch

We have to go with the carbon tax. It's the lesser of two evils. We can get it through, and it has to be done. We can't sit on our hands and do nothing. We have to cop the pain.

Faceless Man 1

Pain, there'll be plenty of that. The Monk will never let up on it. He'll rant and rave and call us liars. I can feel it already.

[Faceless Man 3 enters]

Faceless Man 3

Your majesty, I bring good news and bad news. The good news is that we have done a deal with the old Slipper from the Ming House. He's agreed to be speaker, and he'll support us. That gives us control.

The Black Swan

That's wonderful news. Watch the Mad Monk howl and bitch about that. That's great work, but what's the bad news?

Faceless Man 3

Well you know the cheeky young Naughty Unionist, the smart-arse type. He used to be an official with one of our unions. Well, he's had his hand in the till, spending union money, using it to pay for hookers, living the high life. He's going to face a stack of charges. It looks really bad, and makes us look bad. You know, the Monk will rave on about union crooks.

Simon the Clean

Can we cut him loose, expel him from the party?

The Black Swan

Trouble with that is we need his vote. We can't risk him going over to the dark side.We might have to see if he can hang on for three years, till the next showdown with the Monk.

Winky Bill

We might be able to hold on that long, but it'll cost us a lot of skin. The Monk will have a field day over that and the carbon tax. Plus he's sold his soul to the Rich Mynahs over the mining tax, so they're making trouble for us. On top of that, we'll have fucking MacRudd giving us shit from our own side.

[they all sit around in gloomy silence. Faceless Man 2 leans over the back of a sofa and belches violently]

Scene 2
Outside the Palace

The Mad Monk is yelling into a loud hailer on the back of a truck, alongside the Parrot, several other Reptiles, the Twig Man, the Pilbara Princess, the Big Mynahs and several other Polluters. Some are holding large posters, showing the Red Witch holding a large knife in a stabbing position, and covered in blood.

The Mad Monk

The Red Witch is a liar. A LIAR. She's a LIAR. She's done nothing but LIE, LIE LIE ever since she stabbed MacRudd in the back. She had blood all over her and she tells LIES.

The Pilbara Princess

The carbon tax is a lie. She's nothing but a LIAR.

The Parrot

How can the witch sleep at night, with all her lies. Her parents will die of shame, the way she has disgraced them.

The Reptiles [yelling into their loudhailers]

The Red Witch is a LIAR. LIAR. LIAR. DITCH THE WITCH. DITCH THE WITCH. DITCH THE WITCH. DITCH THE WITCH.

[The chanting continues]

Scene 3
The Throne Room

Gloom pervades the Throne Room. The Faceless Men and the usual suspects are sitting around muttering away.

Lady Gong

And now, on top of their manufactured outrage over the Naughty Unionist, the Mings have pulled out all the stops to knock off the Slipper—the 'Turncoat Slipper' as they call him. They're claiming he's abused travel and other allowances, and that he's sexually abused that young poof in his office. The Monk and that little prick, the Schoolboy Smartarse, are having a field day at our expense.

Faceless Man 1

Oh shit! The great coup was too good to be true. Two dodgy people to make us look bad. What do we do now?

Faceless Man 2

Nothing. Not a fucking thing! The Mad Monk and the Schoolboy Smartarse can carry on all they like. The fact is they're innocent until proven guilty. The wheels of justice grind very slow. Chances are they'll last until the next showdown. By that stage, it won't matter. All we do is say that everyone is entitled to the presumption of innocence, and we'll await the judgement of the courts. Get me another drink.

Winky Bill

OK, so we just hang tough. Our major problem is the way the Mad Monk is raving on all day, every day, about 'This Great Big New Tax'—supported by the Rich Mynahs and the Reptiles.

Lady Gong

That's not the end of our problems. MacRudd is lining up his forces for an attack. He's going to try for a coup in the next couple of weeks. Even Mark the Angry—you know how much he hates MacRudd—has been giving us a hard time.

The Black Swan

MacRudd can try, but he won't have the numbers. By the way, did you like the way the Monk and the Schoolboy Smartarse scampered from the forum yesterday. Like the dogs were after them.

Faceless Man 1

Best laugh I've had in a long time. Anyway, we know MacRudd's coming, so let's shore up our numbers and thrash him. An overwhelming victory, to leave him so damaged that he'll never be able to challenge again. We must absolutely trounce him.

Faceless Man 2

OK, let's get to it. Time to hit the phones. When we're sure the numbers are strong enough, we can bring it on. [takes another gulp]

Faceless Man 3

After we thrash him we make sure everyone comes out and tells the public what an arsehole he is, and how impossible he is to work with. It's what we should have done last time.

Scene 4
The MacRudd Chateau

MacRudd

Those bastards. Those unrepentant, unreconstructed, dirty, slimy, ratfucking cunts! Promising to vote for me, and look what they've done. More than half of those who guaranteed me their vote finished up siding with that fucking witch! And now, the final insult. She's called in old Bob the Blow-In as roving ambassador. She's doing everything she can to humiliate me.

Lady MacRudd

What I'll never forgive is the way so many of them have now come out and said how they hate you and could never work with you. This rubbish that you were impossible to work with. What nonsense. I know how sweet you are, darling, and how lovely you are to work with, all the time.

MacRudd

Well they can forget about having me as their roving ambassador, that's for sure. I'll be outside the tent now, and I'll be free to say whatever I like about them. And I shall! Those arseholes will suffer like never before. I'll bring them down, I promise you. They'll come crawling back to me, begging me to come back and save them. I. WILL. BE. KING. . . . . AGAIN!

Scene 5
Backroom at the Palace

Simon the Clean, Winky Bill, The Earl of Midnight, Lady Gong and the Faceless Men are sitting around, with their heads down. Gloom pervades the room.

Faceless Man 3

These numbers are terrible. We're doomed. There's no way out.

Faceless Man 1

We're getting nowhere. The Red Witch can't get a clear run—and she's getting as paranoid as MacRudd was. We're back in paralysis mode. There's no way we can win unless something drastic happens—a real game-changer. And this story about the Ambulance Chasers has done some damage, even though she did nothing wrong.

Lady Gong

When she made her misogyny speech, I hoped she was getting on top of the Monk, but things turned bad again, very quickly. The Tories have such hatred of her. It's coming from all sides—the Reptiles, the Mad Monk, the Rich Mynahs, the Polluters, the Deniers, there's such a never-ending chorus that she can't make any progress. Plus the bastard MacRudd himself has been doing everything he can to bring her down. I'd bet he planted the Ambulance Chasers story!

Faceless Man 2

It's useless. It's too late. They're in the Fuhrerbunker now, with the Alsatians. There's no talking to them.

Faceless Man 1

Shit, is it that bad? What do we do now?

Faceless Man 2

The only thing left is the . . . [pauses] . . . ***nuclear option***.

Simon the Clean, Winky Bill and *The Earl of Midnight* [in unison]

NO, NO. Anything but that.

Faceless Man 2

Hate it as we all do, there's nothing else. We'll lose for sure if we don't. Sure, we might still lose with the bastard MacRudd, but we probably won't lose as badly. With him, even if we lose, we can rebuild for the future. With the Red Witch, we'll never recover.

Lady Gong

There are so many here who could never support him.

Faceless Man 1

Many of our regional soldiers will feel that they have more hope of defending their territories with him, so they'll probably support him.

Lady Gong

So, I should talk to the queen about this? [pauses] . . . . . . Who's coming with me?

Winky Bill and *Simon the Clean* [together, shrugging their shoulders]

OK. We'll come with you.

Scene 6
The Throne Room

The Red Witch is at her desk, when Lady Gong, Winky Bill and Simon the Clean are ushered in.

The Red Witch

Well, here is a fine triumvirate. What news have you, my friends?

Lady Gong

The news is not good my queen. The fiend MacRudd is readying for a challenge. He calls himself the people's champion. He's determined to be king once more.

The Red Witch

Why am I not surprised? Even though he swore never to challenge again.

Simon the Clean

Well he won't be making a direct challenge. He has supporters who are canvassing on his behalf. He himself is pretending to have nothing to do with it, awaiting the call of the desperate provincials who hope he can save them. His plan is to appear to be reluctant, only returning by popular demand. You know . . . that sort of bullshit.

The Red Witch

Well, let's smoke him out. How about I call on the challenge, and see how much support we each have, and make it clear that the loser retires from public life. That's it—***finito!***

Winky Bill

Good idea, let's do it.

Scene 7
The Palace Courtyard

The Reptiles are gathering. Simon the Clean has called a press conference. There is speculation as to what he will say.

Laurie the Fat Goat [ponderously to TV camera]

The big question is—Does Simon the Clean vote with his conscience or look to what the electorate is saying? We all know that he and his supporters can't stand MacRudd, but they are staring at electoral oblivion with the Red Witch. The polls are showing that the witch will lead her camp to a catastrophic defeat, whereas MacRudd is almost level with the Mad Monk. For the survival of many of his cohorts, Simon the Clean just might swallow his pride and switch his support to MacRudd. Here he comes now. We'll soon find out.

Simon the Clean enters with a few supporters, and walks over behind a phalanx of microphones. TV arc lights come on and photographers get busy, with flashes popping constantly. A few of the Reptiles start throwing questions at him, but Simon holds up his hands and clears his throat.

Simon the Clean

Recent events have given us all in the royal household plenty to think about. I have always been a strong and loyal supporter of the queen, but I have to balance that support against what is best for the kingdom. If nothing changes, we are heading for a disaster, which would enable the Mad Monk to become king. Such a result would devastate the kingdom of Oz, and we must do everything we can to prevent it.

There is clamour from the Reptiles, all shouting to be heard above the others. Simon the Clean holds up a hand, then points at Laurie the Fat Goat.

Laurie the Fat Goat

Simon, does that mean that you're switching your support to MacRudd? For him to return as king?

Simon the Clean

Yes Laurie, I believe if we can unite behind MacRudd, we'll maximise our chances of defeating the Mad Monk, and saving the kingdom from the disaster that he would be as king. I do this with a heavy heart, but in the conviction that this will ultimately be best for the kingdom.

Scene 8
The Palace Courtyard

The same Reptiles are again present twenty-four hours later, speculating on what is happening this time.

Laurie the Fat Goat

Well, after Simon the Clean's declaration yesterday, of support for MacRudd, there has been a lot of commentary, calling for the Red Witch to go.

One of the Reptiles produces a small radio, tuned in to the Parrot's morning talkback program. They listen intently

The Parrot [on the radio]

At long last, the Red Witch is dead. Not before time. This back-stabbing lying witch with blood on her hands, is about to have done to her what she did to MacRudd, and what she has been doing to the kingdom over the last three years. The word is that, after Simon the Clean ditched her yesterday, Winky Bill is about to do the same today. As far as I'm concerned, she can go back to nowhere, where she belongs.

The assembled Reptiles murmur about the Parrot's announcement on the radio.

Laurie the Fat Goat

That's what I've been hearing, too. Winky Bill has called us here, and is expected to join Simon the Clean and a growing list of deserters of the Red Witch. Look, here he comes now.

Winky Bill enters, with a handful of supporters. He stands behind the microphones, and waits for the hubbub to quieten.

Winky Bill

I am here today to tell you where I stand in the contest for the monarchy. You all know that I have supported the queen throughout her reign. Today, I announce that I can no longer do so. [holds up his hands until the clamour dies down] I have to put aside my personal preference in favour of the public good. So I am supporting MacRudd to return to the throne. He is our strongest hope of saving the kingdom from the horrible prospect of the grotesque Mad Monk becoming king.

Scene 9
The MacRudd Chateau

MacRudd and Lady MacRudd are watching Winky Bill's press conference on TV. MacRudd has a smile on his face.

Lady MacRudd

There you are, my darling. You surely have the numbers now. With Simon the Clean and Winky Bill on board, you'll be well over the line. They control enough support for you to be guaranteed a return to the throne. And to be rid of the witch.

MacRudd [scowling]

Don't remind me of that bitch. If she hadn't knifed me, we would never have been in this position. Well may we say 'God Save the Queen' [laughs at his channeling of the Godfather]. Anyway, I'm still nervous. Remember how last time, about two-thirds of the bastards promised me their support, only to fade away to nothing when the pressure was on.

Lady MacRudd

But this time, my love, they're declaring themselves in public. This time is your time!

Scene 10
A Talkback Radio Studio

The Parrot is taking calls. As usual he's doing ninety per cent of the talking.

The Parrot

And now we have Sid from Sydney. What do you want to know Sid?

Sid from Sydney

Is this the end of the witch?

The Parrot

Take my word for it Sid. The wicked witch is dead. Ding dong. All gone. I'm never wrong. The Red Witch is out. Over and out! Except for when they cart her off to jail for that stuff she tried when she was with those crooks, the Ambulance Chasers. Good night, witch.

Sid from Sydney

But . . .

The Parrot

No buts Sid. It's all over for the witch. Serves her right for what she did to MacRudd. Not that he'll be around for long. I'll soon have my man the Mad Monk on the throne. Then we'll settle a few scores. He'll do what he's told, no worries. If he doesn't, we'll find someone else. [starts singing] Ding Dong, the Wicked Witch is dead.

ACT 6
THE RETURN OF THE KING

Scene 1
The Throne Room

MacRudd and Lady MacRudd are exultant. MacRudd is parading around in his crown and ermine robes, and admiring himself in the mirror.

MacRudd

She's gone. The witch is gone. King once more!

Lady MacRudd

Back where you belong, my love. [starts singing] Love takes us back where we belong . . .

MacRudd

Yes, yes, my love. Now we have to deal with the Mad Monk. We're level pegging at the moment, and the momentum is with us. Watch me go now. [yells to his staff] Get me the Faceless Men!

[The Faceless Men have been waiting in the outer chamber, and now come rushing in]

Ah, there you are. We must capitalise on our momentum. What can we do to outdo the Mad Monk?

Faceless Man 1

Well the Mad Monk and the Boat Stopper have been painting us as weak on the refugee issue. Why don't we come up with a solution that's tougher than theirs?

Faceless Man 2

Tougher than theirs? Their plan is inhuman, and breaches all United Nations conventions. How could we be tougher?

MacRudd

No, I like it. They have the Pacific Solution. Let us have solutions everywhere—Malaysia, Manus Island, Nauru. Let's open up everywhere we can find. Yes, do it. Think up whatever you can that's harsher than theirs, and we'll announce it tomorrow! We'll show up that fucking Boat Stopper prick!

Scene 2
The Mad Monk's Office

The Mad Monk is conferring with the White Bishop, the Archbishop, Big Joe the Bean Counter, the Baron of Net Worth and the Boat Stopper.

The Mad Monk

That dopey prick is trying to outdo us on being tough on boat people. What a joke! Hey, Boat Stopper, whatever he does, come up with something tougher. We can always be nastier than him!

The Boat Stopper [laughing]

No problem. They're not in our league there. We'll cream them. You just watch me. 'Let's play rough. MacRudd will be the first to cry "Enough"'.

The White Bishop

We're also on a winner with Bob the Blow-In. His ego is nearly as big as MacRudd's. He's upsetting people all over the world.

The Mad Monk

Right. Bring on the showdown.This is gunna be good!

Scene 3
The Throne Room

MacRudd is pacing around, yelling at everyone. The Faceless Men are poring over reams of paperwork, and mumbling among themselves.

MacRudd

What's wrong with you people? You should be celebrating. I have saved you. We're going to have a glorious victory.

Faceless Man 3

Not on these numbers we're not.

MacRudd

What do you mean? The people love me.

Faceless Man 1

The numbers are going south. Fast! We'll be savaged at the showdown.

MacRudd

But . . . but we'll do better than we would have if the witch was still queen won't we? [pleading] Won't we?

Faceless Man 1 [raises his eyebrows as he looks at the other Faceless Men]

Y.. Y..Yes, yes. Much Better. Of course!

ACT 7
THE ROUT

Scene 1
The Throne Room

The new king and his retinue are lolling about, drinking champagne. They are very convivial and mellow.

The Mad Monk

Here we are, my friends. Didn't I tell you I'd take you here? How sweet it is. Just think—I've vanquished both MacRudd and the Red Witch. The enemy has been slaughtered. They're leaderless, and completely dispirited.

The White Bishop [laughing]

The whisper is that they'll have poor old Winky Bill as their leader. [there are screams of laughter] Stop laughing, it's true. Poor old Bill. He'll be a very lonely man.

Big Joe the Bean Counter

This will be a walk in the park. They have nobody—and no policies. I just wish our old Squire wasn't doing their work for them.

The Boat Stopper

The Squire? That old windbag. He's just like the other old kings—can't stand not being the centre of attention. He's past it. Don't waste your time on him.

The Mad Monk

Wonder if I'll be like that in my dotage? Spouting off about everything and nothing. Are there any barnacles we need to scrape off?

The Boat Stopper

There'll be a couple of minor headaches while we clean up the last remnants of opposition, and a couple of the Fairies at the Bottom of the Garden, but after that, we're clear. Old Dr Green is history. The Browns will be a rabble without him.

The Baron of Net Worth

We'll still have to deal with the Big Dog and his Puppies, but they'll go along with our plans. The Dog will make some noise, and get his face in the media, but his interests are much the same as ours.

Scene 2
The Palace Grounds

Enter the three witches. They are all wearing black and very downcast. One carries a bucket and mop, another has a broomstick over her shoulder, and the third has a rolled-up banner. Part words 'Fee' and '..asers' are visible from the banner. The witches are moaning.

The Witches [in unison]

Oh woe
How tragic it has been
Our girl was on the throne
But is no longer queen

MacRudd has schemed and spat
Our red has been destroyed
And then, to cap it off
We're cast into the void

The kingdom is condemned
The Monk's astride the throne
Full of bile and hate
Our hopes have all been blown

So now, what can we do?
Whither goes our Red?
Outcast by her defeat
Where can she lay her head?

Friendless all are we
Our future all torn down
As sadness tears the witch
Who once did wear the crown

Moaning still, they exit the stage

ACT 8
EXILE

Scene 1
The MacRudd Chateau

MacRudd and Lady MacRudd are miserable. The reality of defeat is just sinking in.

MacRudd

Those ungrateful bastards have turned on me again. Blaming me for losing at the showdown. Ingrates.

Lady MacRudd

If it wasn't for you, my love, they'd have been totally routed. You saved many of the territories for them.

MacRudd

So now they have Winky Bill for a so-called leader. Poor old dull old Winky. A very poor substitute for me. I'll hang around for a little while, then leave Oz and take over the United Nations.

Lady MacRudd

Are you sure the Mad Monk will support you?

MacRudd

Of course he will. He owes me big time. He wouldn't be king now if I hadn't brought the witch down. And remember the way I've helped the White Bishop deal with people all over the world. Oh yes, they'll support me!

Scene 2
The Forum

The Archbishop is ruling the People's Forum with an enthusiastic but heavy hand. She is smiling and nodding to the new king, and responding to all his questions with 'Yes, Your Majesty" and "Of course, Your Majesty". She is very severe, however, on the rump that sits opposite him

The Archbishop

Order! The honourable member is out of order.

Winky Bill

Madam Speaker . . . .

The Archbishop

Don't you dare call me Madam Speaker. I have declared myself to be the Queen of Hearts, so you must call me 'Your Highness' or I'll throw you out of here. Just like I've thrown out thirty-three of your colleagues already today. I'm on track for a personal best today! [preening herself]

Winky Bill

Thank you Your Highness, I was coming to that. Why is it that, since the new king has occupied the throne, you have evicted my followers over three hundred times, but not one of his?

The Archbishop

I rule this chamber. Don't you understand? If I choose to call myself the Queen of Hearts, then that's who I am. If you disagree with me, I'll throw you out, just like the others. I make the rules here. And I can change them. Whenever I like!

Winky Bill

But..

The Archbishop

Don't you 'But' me. [yells] ORF WITH HIS HEAD. Take him away. [smiles] Don't worry, my dear. I just like saying that. As commander of this chamber, I have chosen to define the expression 'Orf with his head' to mean that you are suspended from the Forum for two sitting days. So that's all it means. Out you go, out you go.

Scene 3
The MacRudd Chateau

MacRudd and Lady MacRudd are sitting at home, looking forlorn and miserable.

MacRudd

Look—there's a report that Big Joe has written an autobiography. He really fancies himself. What a bag of piss. Reciting all his achievements? It must be the smallest book ever published!

Lady MacRudd

Cheer up my darling. The People were too stupid to understand how good you were. You're better off without them. We can now concentrate on increasing our wealth, and plan on getting you the top job at the United Nations. Oz was always too small minded for your abilities. The rest of the world is moving on climate change now anyway.

MacRudd

You're right of course, my love. You know that my new best friend is the White Bishop. She's the only one of the Mad Monk's crew who is doing OK, thanks to all the advice I've given her. She might even finish up as queen—wouldn't that be a hoot?

Lady MacRudd

Just as long as she remembers to support your claim to the top job at the United Nations.

MacRudd

And the Mad Monk is all over the place. That fucking Boat Stopper is trying to take over the whole country. I hear that everyone there hates his guts. He's getting all the publicity.

Lady MacRudd

Yes, he's so arrogant, he makes the Schoolboy Smartarse look almost dignified.

[MacRudd's phone rings]

MacRudd

Hello my dear White Bishop. How nice of you to call. When will you be announcing your support? [pauses] . . . . WHAT? ARE YOU FUCKING JOKING? THAT PRANCING POOF? YOU FUCKING TURNCOAT. LYING. BACKSTABBING.. ARSEHOLES!! [sobbing, terminates the call]

Lady MacRudd

My darling, what is it?

MacRudd [apoplectic with rage, and almost speechless]

Those . . . those unspeakable, shitty, slimy bastards have turned on me—just like everyone else . . . . They . . . they've dropped my claim, and . . . . and instead they've nominated the fucking old Sundowner.

Lady MacRudd

The Sundowner?

MacRudd

You know, their old roving ambassador from years ago. The old poofy bastard with the plummy accent. Fucking fishnet stockings and all that. Fancy him at the UN!

Lady MacRudd [picks up the remote control and turns on the TV]

Let's change the subject, my love. I'll find something here to take your mind off all that nonsense.

MacRudd

Look, here's a story on fossil fuels. That'll fuck the Mad Monk. Let's listen to what he has to say for himself now.

The Mad Monk [on TV]

Yes, coal is essential for the prosperity of Oz, and the prosperity of the world for many decades to come.

MacRudd collapses, screaming and tearing at his hair . . .

Epilogue

Enter the Silver Bodgie and the Master Blaster. The Silver Bodgie is carrying a scroll

The Silver Bodgie

Argghhhhh . . . .

This tale of King MacRudd
a tragedy of this age
the spillage of his blood
his temper, fury, rage

From such a wondrous start
his flaws have been so bad
they've broken this old heart
and made me feel so sad

The Apology went well
and our high flying king
sounded the death knell
for leaders of the Ming

But come with power drunk
MacRudd then lost his edge
and up against the Monk
he threw us off the ledge

And when the witch was queen
he leaked and stabbed and spun
destroyed what might have been
and gave the Monk his run

The Master Blaster

We talk of the vision thing
for those who wear the crown
when it's absent in the king
it all comes crashing down

We lie wounded in the mud
and the Monk now proudly reigns
O cursed be MacRudd
the cause of all our pains!

[aside, to the Sliver Bodgie, as they exit the stage]
Would never have happened in our day, Bob . . . .

Printed in Australia
AUOC02n0848090615
268092AU00001B/1/P

9 781942 703044